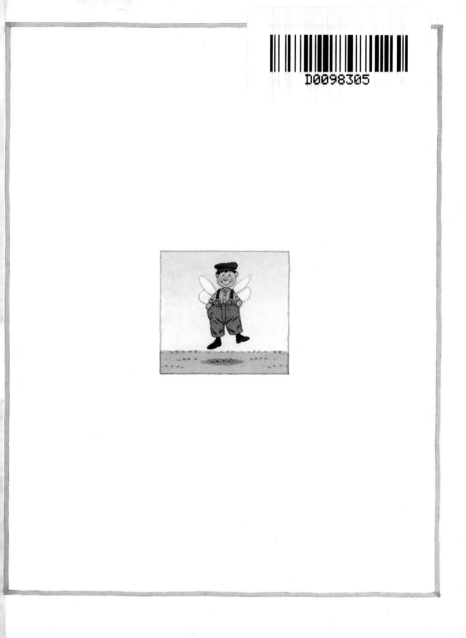

The Usborne
Little Book
of
Fairy Stories

Written and retold by Philip Hawthorn
Illustrated by Stephen Cartwright

Designed by Amanda Barlow
Edited by Jenny Tyler
Cover designed by Hannah Ahmed

This edition first published in 2002 by Usborne Publishing Ltd,
Usborne House, 83-85 Saffron Hill, London EC1N 8RT
www.usborne.com

Printed in Italy.

CONTENTS

There is a little yellow duck in each story. Can you find it?

POLLY AND THE PIXIES

Polly was on a very important journey. There wasn't a moment to lose, so she was walking as fast as she could. On her way past a small village green, she noticed the villagers lounging around.

"Why's a little girl like you in such a big rush?" asked a woman.

"I've just been to market to sell a gold ring," said Polly. "My mother's ill, and we need money to help make her better."

"Well, you'd go a lot quicker with a nice, refreshing drink inside you," said a man. He offered her a full glass. "Here, a present from the village."

Polly was so hot, she took the glass and drank thirstily.

When she'd finished, they produced another, and another, and another. After her fourth glass she said, "Excuse me, where's the toilet?"

An old woman said, "This way my dear. It's all right, you can leave your bag. We'll look after it for you." The other villagers nodded.

When she got back Polly thanked them, picked up her bag and set off. When she was outside the village she looked into her bag, and her stomach turned to jelly. The bag was full of stones.

"I've been robbed!" she wailed, and burst into tears. The sound of tears falling on the ground woke a fairy who was asleep nearby.

"What's the matter?" she asked, yawning. Polly told her how the villagers had stolen her money. "That village is know to be the meanest in the country. In fact we call the people who live there the Nasties," said the fairy. "This is a job for the pixies!"

She blew into a bluebell flower. In a second they were surrounded by scores of pixies with turned up noses and pointed ears.

"Who be using the pixie horn?" asked one.

"Me," replied the fairy. "Polly here needs your help."

The pixies murmured worriedly.

"I know you don't like helping humans," continued the fairy. "But if you help Polly you might get a chance to play a trick on the Nasties." At this, the pixies started pulling at their beards with excitement.

"Tell them your story, Polly," encouraged the fairy. Polly took a deep breath and told the pixies exactly what had happened to her.

When she had finished, the pixie chief said, "Me thinks it's time for a pixie fair."

"A *pixie fair*! A *pixie fair*!" chorused the others.

"What's a pixie fair?" asked Polly.

The chief pixie replied, "Well now, it be a fair held by pixies." They all laughed and pulled each other's beards. "We sets up our stalls, and we sells pixie things like this." Polly watched as he picked up a pine cone and swirled it around very fast. When he opened his hand, the cone had turned into pure gold.

"Here," he said, throwing it to her. "A present from the pixies."

"A *pixie gift*! A *tricksy gift*!" sang the others, and disappeared.

In the time it took Polly to put the gold pine cone in her pocket, the pixies had reappeared, bringing with them the most beautiful stalls.

"What are you going to sell?" asked Polly.

"We *sell, we sell, whatever we sell!*" the pixies sang, and started to hunt around the clearing. They used their magic to turn pieces of tree bark into chunks of gold, spiders' webs into the finest spun silver, and drops of dew into sparkling diamonds. In no time at all the stalls were groaning with precious things.

Meanwhile, back at the village, the Nasties were counting out Polly's money. When they heard the pixies approaching, they quickly hid it.

"*Come to the fair! Come to the fair!*" chanted the pixies. Then they started to dance around the startled people, singing,

> "*Flobbity-wee and flibbity-woo,*
> *A pixie fair we have for you,*
> *With gold and silver, diamonds too,*
> *Come to the pixie fair!*"

The villagers had heard about little people and how they had secret stores of gold. Sensing the chance to make themselves even richer, they picked up their ill-gotten money and followed the pixies.

When they saw the stalls their eyes goggled with greed. The pixies cleverly charged such bargain prices that the villagers spent all their money. As the last villager struggled off with her bulging bag of pixie riches, the fairy led Polly out from where they'd been hiding.

"But why did you sell your things so cheaply?" protested Polly. "They don't deserve to have all that after what they did to me." At this the pixies laughed loudly.

"How much would you pay for an old leaf?" said the chief.

"I beg your pardon?" replied Polly.

"*Look! Look! Lookety-look!*" shouted the pixies, pointing at one of the gold leaves that was left on a stall. Polly looked and saw the gold leaf change back into a normal leaf.

"Do you mean all those precious things will turn into ordinary things again?" asked Polly.

"*She's bright, she's bright as a moonlit night!*" sang the pixies.

"And we've got all your money back," said the fairy. "Come on you pixies, hand it over."

The pixies gave Polly most of the money, keeping a bit for themselves. (Pixies aren't that nice.) Then they gathered together and sang,

"*Farewell! Farewell And a fare thee well!*" and with one last chuckle, they were gone.

"Now," said the fairy, "I think you'd better be going home too." There was a bright flash, and Polly found herself at her mother's bedside. Her mother looked up and smiled.

"Did you sell the ring?" she asked.

"I *did*! I *did*! I *diddly-did*!" sang Polly, smiling back. She reached into her pocket and pulled out the money and the gold pine cone.

The pine cone never turned back, but all the Nasties' things did. If you go to the village today, they'll boast about the time they all bought pixie gold, but they won't show you any of it. And you'll know why, won't you?

ANGEL

There was once a fairy girl called Angel, who wasn't at all like an angel. She was both proud and spiteful. One day, Angel was out playing hide-and-seek with her friend, Flutterby. This was good fun because they were able to make themselves as small as they liked. Angel was hiding in a daffodil when she heard footsteps. Thinking it was Flutterby, she leapt out, making herself bigger.

"BOO!" she shouted, and laughed. But her laughter soon stopped, for right in front of her was a human boy. Angel disappeared instantly, but she knew she'd been seen.

"Ugh! A human!" she said to herself. "Double ugh! A human *boy*! I expect he thinks he's really clever to have seen me, but I'll show him."

She spent a few days watching out for the boy, and it wasn't long before she saw him coming home from school. She followed him to where he lived, then went back to her mother. She had a plan ...

"Mother," she said, innocently. "If anyone hurt me, would you be angry?"

"Yes," said her mother.

"Would you punish them?" asked Angel.

"Yes I would, why?" replied her mother.

"Oh, er ... nothing," said Angel, and she flew off.

That night, the little boy was getting ready for bed when down the chimney flew Angel.

"Hello little boy," she said.

"Oh, hello," he said, recognizing Angel at once.

"Do you want to be friends?" asked Angel, smiling a little too sweetly.

"All right," said the boy.

"Good. What's your name?"

The boy was much more clever than Angel thought, and he was on his guard.

"My name is Me Myself," he said, though it wasn't of course.

"What a stupid name," thought Angel. "What a lovely name," she said. "Let's play chase. Catch me!"

She started flitting about the room. The boy hadn't a chance of catching her as she was so light and quick. But after a minute or two, the naughty fairy fell to the floor, holding her knee.

"Ooohh!" she wailed. "You hurt me, you clumsy human boy."

"I didn't touch you, he said, truthfully.

"Yes you did! Yes you did! Yes you DID!" said Angel. "I'm going to tell. MO-THER!"

Now fairies have amazingly good hearing, and in the flicker of a candle Angel's mother arrived on the roof of the house.

"What's the matter, Angel?" she called down the chimney.

"Someone's hurt my kneeee," she whined.

"Are you angry?"

"Yes I am," replied her mother.

"Will you punish them?" she asked.

"Yes. Who did it?" came the reply.

Angel glared at the human boy and smiled vengefully. "The person who hurt my knee was Me Myself," she shouted.

"I see," called her mother. "Well, if it was you yourself, then I will have to punish you yourself."

She waved her magic wand. Before Angel could realize that the boy had outsmarted her, she found herself back in her own bedroom. Angel's mother kept her promise, and her naughty daughter wasn't allowed out for a week. Angel wasn't quite so eager to play tricks after that.

THE HAIRY BOGGART

George Flaxstead was an honest farmer, who just about managed to earn a living. One evening, on his way home, he met the mega-mischievous Hairy Boggart.

"I wants a chit-chat," it said. George Flaxstead knew that boggarts meant trouble and that he'd have to find a way to get rid of it, but he was far too hungry to think now. "Come back in the morning," he said. The boggart left, grumbling.

After George Flaxstead had eaten his supper he thought carefully, and eventually came up with a good plan.

Next day, he found the boggart looking greedily at his field.

"Goodsome land," said the creature. "Grow lovely-jubbly grub for tummy-rumbly boggart."

"There's enough for us both," said George Flaxstead. "We'll go halves on the next harvest, and that's my final offer." The boggart was too lazy to argue, so it agreed.

"Do you want the tops or the bottoms?" said George Flaxstead.

"Umm, topsies," replied the boggart. "Bye-bye, see you at harvest." And it went.

The clever farmer planted a field of potatoes. So when the boggart returned at harvest time, it got the useless leafy tops, and the farmer kept all the lovely plump potatoes which grew underground.

"Next time I want the bottomsies," growled the Hairy Boggart. And it went.

The farmer now planted the field with wheat. So when the boggart again returned at harvest time, it got the useless dry stalks while George Flaxstead got lots of golden grains of wheat.

The boggart was even more angry. " You skillywig!" it said, jumping up and down. "Next year, you grows corn. We cuts corn together and reapers-keepers what we cut.

The boggart was much stronger than George Flaxstead, so it would be able to harvest most of the crop, leaving the poor farmer to starve.

But George soon had another plan.

The next day before the corn harvest, he bought some iron rods from the village blacksmith. After he had painted them golden yellow to match his crop, he stuck them in one end of the field.

The boggart arrived the next day. "Right, ready steady?" it said, sharpening its scythe. "We keeps what we reaps."

"You start over there," said the farmer, pointing to the end with the iron stalks of corn.

The boggart started strongly enough, but then found it tough going. The iron stalks, being so difficult to cut, made it tire very quickly, and they blunted the scythe.

"Getting tired?" taunted George Flaxstead. The Hairy Boggart snarled and gave a huge swipe at the corn. Its scythe snapped, and so did its temper. As it ran off, roaring loudly, George Flaxstead chuckled and shouted after him in his best boggart voice, "Me no scary, hairy fairy." After that, he was never ever bothered by boggarts again.

THE ENDLESS STORY

Orlando lived by the sea, and liked to spend time in its company. One evening, he was walking along the beach when he saw a young girl sitting on a rock, combing her hair. As he got closer, he saw that she was a mermaid. Hearing his footsteps, she jumped with surprise.

"You have seen me in the last light of the day," she said. "Now I must grant you a wish. Take this comb and come back at this time tomorrow. Comb the waves and I will come to you. But don't tell anyone you have seen me." Then she slipped silently into the sea and was gone.

That night, Orlando was having a drink with some sailors. As is often the case when men get together, they were boasting by telling amazing stories of the sea.

When it was Orlando's turn he did something very silly. Pulling out the comb he said, "This belongs to a mermaid. Tomorrow I'll have a wish granted." The others laughed scornfully.

"Come and see, if you don't believe me," he said.

So the next evening, Orlando went to the sea's edge. The others crouched behind a fishing boat. Orlando combed the water, and the mermaid rose to meet him. At once the other men rushed forward and grabbed her, shouting things like, "Give us a wish, sweetheart."

Suddenly, they heard a loud roar, and Orlando and the sailors found themselves in Undersea Fairyland. In front of them stood Neptune, king of the sea fairies.

"You have dared to capture a mermaid," said Neptune. "I will release you only if you can tell me a story that never ends."

The sailors each tried to tell the longest tale they could, but no matter how hard they tried to spin out their stories, they eventually dried up.

Finally, it was Orlando's turn. He thought of his walks along the beach, then he began.

"A man decided to polish the beach. He picked up the first grain of sand and polished that, then he picked up the third grain of sand and polished that ..."

Orlando carried on telling how, one at a time, each grain of sand was polished.

When he got to the two hundred and sixty-fifth grain, Neptune said,

"All right, that's enough. I'll let you off this time, but you've been warned." He waved his huge trident and Orlando vanished back to the beach. He never saw the mermaid again, or had his wish.

As for the sailors who had been left behind, Neptune stared at them and said, "You couldn't tell me the story I wanted to hear, so let me tell you one."

He sat down and began to retell Orlando's story about polishing grains of sand. And he went on and on and on and on, far past the part where he'd stopped Orlando. He went on endlessly.

Orlando's story wasn't all that good, was it? That's because good stories come to an end ...
... like this one.

SNIFFER

There were two things that Sniffer always had: a purple silk handkerchief and a cold. That was why he was called Sniffer, because his cold made him sniff all the time.

One Thursday, Sniffer was going to market near Dublin in Ireland. He wanted to buy some vegetables for supper. "I wish I had more money to buy meat for a change. My wife's forgotten what meat tastes like. I'd love to cook some for her," he sighed.

After walking a few more miles, he heard a strange sound from behind a hedge. He peeped through it and saw a small man sitting on the ground, mending a shoe. Sniffer looked at the man and suddenly realized that he was a leprechaun.

Sniffer immediately remembered his grandmother's advice. "If you ever see a leprechaun, catch hold of him," she had said. "Don't let go, and don't take your eyes off him for a second, or he'll be off with a laugh and a tickle. Ask him where his pot of gold is buried, and he'll have to tell you."

So Sniffer waited until the leprechaun reached into his bag for another nail, then he made his move.

"Gotcha!" he called, as his hand tightened around the leprechaun's arm. He was surprised that the leprechaun just laughed.

"Ah!" That's caught me well and good, so it has," he giggled. "To be sure you've got the better of me."

"Yes," replied Sniffer, a little uneasily. "Now I want your pot of gold."

"Well, if you just let go of my arm, I'll lead you to it." Sniffer started to loosen his grip, then remembered his grandmother's warning not to let go. "I know what you're up to," he said, and he held on even more tightly.

"Well now, if you aren't the smartest lad in Ireland," said the leprechaun. "I reckon you're so smart you'd always help a beautiful girl in trouble."

"Of course I would," said Sniffer.

"Well, there's one behind you who's being chased by a ferocious bull," said the little man, pointing over Sniffer's shoulder.

Sniffer was about to turn around when he again remembered the advice his grandmother had given him not to look away.

"You little pickle," said Sniffer, staring at the leprechaun even harder. "Now, it's gold time!"

The leprechaun started out across the field, trying without success to wriggle himself free. By now, Sniffer was sniffing quite a bit because he hadn't been able to blow his nose while holding onto the leprechaun. Eventually, they arrived in the middle of a huge field of beautiful poppies.

"It's under this poppy," said the leprechaun, pointing to one. "Dig down deep and you'll find the gold."

"I just need to go and get a spade," said Sniffer. "How will I know which is the right flower when I get back?"

"I'll wait here and tell you," the leprechaun replied, his eyes growing brighter.

"I'm not falling for that," said Sniffer. At this point, he decided to blow his nose. He reached into his pocket and pulled out the purple silk handkerchief. Then a thought came to him.

"Tie this handkerchief to the poppy," Sniffer said. The leprechaun did as he was told.

"Promise me that you won't take if off. Cross your heart and hope to die, or whatever leprechauns say."

"I promise," said the leprechaun.

"Right," said Sniffer. Then he let go of the leprechaun and ran off to his house.

When he got back to the field, he saw that the leprechaun had not removed the silk handkerchief. What he had done was tie identical handkerchiefs to all the other poppies in the field. It would take years to dig under all of them.

"Oh cabbage," said Sniffer. But at least he now had hundreds of silk handkerchiefs. He gathered them all together and put them in the bag he'd brought for the gold.

He then went to the market, where simply by selling three of the silk handkerchiefs he was able to earn enough money to buy a nice piece of meat and some vegetables, which he cooked for his wife that night. And he still had hundreds of silk handkerchiefs left – which was not to be sniffed at.

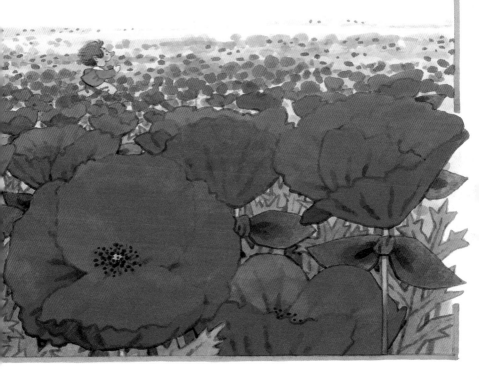

BRAVE WORDS INDEED

Charlie Chumpchop, the shepherd, had left his flock in the care of a friend and gone off for a good walk. As he walked along, he saw a small flute on the ground. He picked it up. It was silver, and so fine that it weighed hardly anything. He put it to his lips and blew. There came the sweetest, purest note you could imagine, and a tiny fairy appeared.

"Can I have my flute back please?" she said. Charlie handed it over.

"Ha! You could have asked for anything," said the fairy. "Don't you know I am bound to reward you? But since you are an honest boy, I will give you something." She reached into her pocket and gave Charlie three small, round, white things. "These are magimints. When you eat one, it will give you exactly the right words to say."

Then she put the flute to her lips and disappeared, leaving the trace of a fairy tune in the still morning air.

Charlie put the magimints into his pocket and headed for the city. At the palace there was a lot of activity.

"I suppose they're having a royal lunch," he thought, looking at the array of noblemen arriving on dashing horses. He went closer and found himself outside a room in which the important guests were talking excitedly.

"You're just in time, sir," said a guard, ushering Charlie into the room and closing the door behind him. The conversation stopped, and twenty pairs of eyes stared at Charlie; stares that would pierce steel.

"What do you want?" said a tall knight in gold tights.

"I... I..." stammered Charlie.

"The poster does say *anyone* can try for the princess' hand," said a fat lord in a fur-trimmed coat, indicating the poster on the door. As conversation began again, Charlie read the poster. This is what it said:

HIS ROYAL MAJESTY KING ROLLMOP III
SEEKS A HUSBAND FOR HIS DAUGHTER,
HER ROYAL HIGHNESS PRINCESS SALAMI.
A TEST WILL BE SET ON THURSDAY NEXT.
ANYONE IS WELCOME.

"That seems a bit unfair on the princess," thought Charlie. "Oh well, I bet I'm as strong and fast as any of this bunch." Then he saw some small writing at the bottom.

UNSUCCESSFUL CANDIDATES WILL BE EXECUTED.

"Executed!" yelled Charlie.

"Oh, don't worry," said a kindly baron. "We all have armies, the king wouldn't dare harm us."

"But the only army I've got is an army of sheep," thought Charlie in dismay. Before he could think of escape, the trumpeter next to him blew a fanfare which made Charlie jump. Some big doors opened, and in came the king and princess. They sat down on their thrones.

The king had a small moustache which twitched nervously. The princess looked incredibly sulky. She was the sort of person who never showed enthusiasm for anything.

"My lords," said the king. "I have decided that the princess shall marry whoever can say the bravest words. Is that all right, my dear?" He looked at Princess Salami.

"Don't care," she said, without the slightest interest.

"And, of course, the rest of you will die," continued the king. "Who's first?"

A rather thin man called Baron Waste stepped up. "I could slay a fierce dragon with my trusty sword."

The next, Sir Dean Tynne, said, "I could slay two
fierce dragons with my knife." Each of those that
followed tried to outdo those before him. Then Count
Üptaten said, "I could slay a hundred huge, hungry
dragons armed only with a small twig and a paper
cup."

The king glanced at his yawning daughter. There
were only two people left.

The first, Sir Pryze, stepped forward. He was tall,
handsome and very rich. "My words of bravery are not
human. For what could be braver than the words of
the king of the beasts, the lion. Grrrrrrrrrr!" And he
growled fiercely. During the applause, the princess
yawned again.

"You boy," said the king, pointing at Charlie.
"You're last."

Charlie walked up to the throne. His face was
frozen in panic, his throat was dry and his knees
were like jelly.

Suddenly, he remembered the magimints the fairy had given him. He put one into his mouth.

"Your Majesty," he began. All at once, it felt as if his tongue had a mind of its own. "Did you hear about the dragon who was in a film? She became very flame-ous."

There was a shocked silence. "Oh dear, maybe that magimint had gone stale," thought Charlie, popping another one into his mouth. Immediately, he said, "Did you hear about the lord who was chased by a lion? He was Lord Claude Bottom."

"How dare you!" bellowed the king. He was just about to order Charlie's immediate execution when he heard a sound that made him stop.

The princess was laughing, so hard that tears were pouring down her cheeks. The king had never seen her laugh before.

"You have always tried to impress me," she said, giggling. "At last someone has made me happy."

"Come to think of it, telling jokes was incredibly brave ... you win, my boy," the king said.

So Charlie and the princess were married, and lived happily for many years.

THE BATH ASSAULT

Wexon-by-Glade was a pretty country town. It was well-known for its neat streets and tidy parks, and as the home of Blubberbelly Bath Salts. Mr. Blubberbelly was fat and rude, unpopular and selfish, and his heart was as hard as cement; but he did make the best bath salts in the country. "Only sensational smells," he'd boast.

The River Glade, which ran behind Mr. Blubberbelly's factory, did not smell very nice however. It had a strange green tinge, with bubbles floating on the top. The fish were often ill, and so were the river sprites who looked after it. In the end two of them went to see Oberon, king of the fairies.

"It's not fair," said Pondweed. "We try to look after the river and everything that lives in, on or by it."

"The situation is very, very bad," said Ripple.

"I know," said Oberon. "I think we should go and have a look around Mr. Blubberbelly's factory."

"But he only makes sensational smells," said Ripple. "It says so on the front."

"We'll see," said the king.

They made themselves invisible, flew into the factory, and came to a noisy room with a large boiling tub and lots of pipes and tubes.

34

There was a wonderful smell of lemon in the room.

"This is the room where they make the bath salts," said Oberon. Then he led them through a door marked 'Waste Room'. The smell was terrible.

"Yukkity ugh!" said the sprites once inside.

"You see, whatever you make, there's always waste," began Oberon, "It's like with cooking. You can make the tastiest food, but there's always something such as carrot tops, onion skins or egg shells, to get rid of. Let's see what Mr. Blubberbelly does with the waste from his factory, shall we?"

They found a pipe which ran out of the room and followed it. It wound around lots of corners and eventually went outside. From the end, thick gunk was pouring straight into the river.

"Stinky-poo!" said Pondweed.

"It's time to have a word with Mr. Blubbersmelly," said Oberon. So that night, the three fairies visited the factory owner in his house. "How dare you come in here!" he shouted. "I'm just about to have my bath. I want to try out my new lemon bath salts. Buzz off." (Mr. Blubberbelly looked soft, but his heart was as hard as cement.)

Now it doesn't do to shout at a fairy, especially if he's a king. Oberon waved a magic spell over the new bath salts and led the fairies away.

"What was the spell, your Majesty?" asked Ripple.

"Wait until tomorrow," came the reply.

Early the next morning, the fairies flew to the market square, and what they saw there made them gasp. Mr. Blubberbelly was sitting in a bath of cement.

"I changed the bath salts to cement powder," said Oberon. "When he mixed it with water and sat in it, it set. Then just for good measure, I made it move over here." They flew down and perched on the bath taps.

"You did this to me!" fumed Mr. Blubberbelly. "I can't move!"

"You expect nice clean water in your bath," said Oberon. "The river creatures expect the same in their river. Only you can help them."

"Never!" said the arrogant man. "I'm not going to be ordered around by a bunch of fairies."

"Suit yourself," said Oberon as they flew away. "You'll only be free when you've found a way to say you're sorry."

Mr. Blubberbelly folded his arms. "I shall not be moved," he shouted.

"You're right there," said a woman on her way to work. "It'd take an elephant to move that bath." Then she called to the others, "Look at old Blubberguts!" Soon, there was a crowd of people looking and laughing at him.

This went on all morning. At lunchtime he started to feel hungry. In the afternoon, he was hungry, cold and bursting to use the toilet.

"All right," he yelled as night fell. "I give in! You win!" But there was no one around. "I know how awful the river is! I will change things, I promise!" But all that could be heard was the wind whistling around the town hall tower.

In the end, he started to cry. As the tears fell onto the cement, they melted it. He climbed out of the sludgy bath and walked home. Next day, he arranged for trucks to take away all the factory waste.

Mr. Blubberbelly's heart remained generous and kind. It had been hard as cement, but now it was melted.

THE TOOTH FAIRY

A lice liked collecting things. Unfortunately they were things that made her parents say, "Oh please! Really, Alice!" For example, she had the two stitches from when she'd cut her chin, a dead beetle she'd found in the bath, and lots more. She kept everything in matchboxes, wrapped in tissue paper. Her father called them her horror boxes.

When a tooth fell out, however, there was no way she'd keep it: teeth were for the tooth fairy.

One evening, Alice sat in her room wiggling a loose tooth with her tongue and wrapped her Aunt Megan's birthday present (a bar of strawberry soap). Aunt Megan always spent her birthday with Alice's family. Aunt Megan was posh and loud, wore lots of make-up and gave the most disgusting kisses. She hated the horror boxes even more than Alice's parents.

The doorbell rang and Alice's mother shouted up the stairs, "Al-ice! Come and say hello to your aunt!"

Alice flumped down the stairs. Excited grown-up babblings were already in full swing, and as she appeared Aunt Megan gushed, "And here's dear Alice. Haven't you grown!"

Alice winced and thought, "Of course. That's what children do."

"Come and give your auntie a kiss," said Aunt Megan. Alice saw the big, pink lips coming towards her, and then ... Slurpy-Slobber! Perfume-Smelly! Sticky-Wet kiss. Eeyuurrgh!

The force of the kiss made not one, but both of Alice's front teeth come out. She used her tongue to explore the new warm holes in her gums. Then she spat the teeth into her hand and held them under her aunt's nose.

"Aunt Megan, look what your kith did!" she lisped. Aunt Megan did look, and turned pale.

"Oh my goodness!" she wailed. "How re-volt-ing!" Then, with a sweep of her hand she sent the teeth flying to the floor. While the grown-ups went to recover with cups of tea, Alice picked up the teeth and went to her room.

She was furiously thinking. "How dare Aunt Megan treat my teeth like that," when she had an idea. She put one tooth under her pillow. Then she unwrapped the soap, put the bloodiest tooth in a matchbox, and wrapped it up. "Happy Birthday, Aunt Dragon," she said. And climbed into bed.

Alice woke in the night feeling even more fed up, and decided to put the other tooth in Aunt Megan's present too. She reached under her pillow and, to her great surprise, grabbed a tiny hand. As she brought it out, a silver glow appeared. It was a fairy, carrying Alice's tooth and a sack.

"You're the tooth fairy," said Alice. "How you glow."

"Of course. That's what fairies do," said the fairy. Pointing at the tooth she said, "Nice one."

"What happenth to the teeth you take?" lisped the front-toothless Alice.

"I'll show you," said the fairy. She took Alice's hand and they both flew out of the window.

To start with, they visited the bedrooms of sleeping children. The fairy disappeared under each pillow with a silver coin and emerged with a tooth, which she put in her sack. Then they flew to the North Pole, to collect a baby polar bear's tooth from under it's pillow of snow. And finally, to a smoky-hot mountain for a huge dragon's tooth which lay under a pillow of hot coals.

"What do you do with the teeth?" said Alice.
"Come on, I'll show you," said the fairy.

They flew for ages, then the fairy started to dive. They were heading for the middle of a ring of mushrooms in a field. Nearer and nearer, faster and faster they got, until Alice was so scared she closed her eyes.

"Hold on tight!" called the fairy.

Scrunch! Whizz! Fizz! Whoooosh!

Alice opended her eyes. The moon seemed enormous, and the stars winked and twinkled brightly. The trees glowed in the moonlight and the rivers looked like liquid silver.

"Welcome to Fairyland," replied to tooth fairy.

The air was as fresh as mountain air, but warm as a summer's evening. As they flew, Alice felt as if she would always be this happy. They soon came to a brightly lit house and looked through a window at the frantic activity inside.

"What'th going on?" said Alice.

"Well, I'm not *the* tooth fairy, I'm *a* tooth fairy. There are lots of us. Come on," said the fairy, and they went inside. "We wash all the teeth in here," she said, pointing to a huge bath. They went into the next room. "This is where the most important thing happens. Watch."

The clean teeth were put into a pot and the lid closed. The fairies gathered around. They pointed their fingers at the pot and sang a fairy song. Soon, the air shimmered with magic. Alice had never seen anything so totally exciting. When the pot was uncovered, it was full of dazzling, shiny pearls.

"We're the only fairies with this magic," said the tooth fairy, proudly. "In this pot were the teeth of rich children and poor children, good children and naughty children. Yet each one has made a perfect pearl. Out of the ordinary comes the amazing!"

Alice had breakfast with the tooth fairies, then it was time to go. She waved goodbye, and as they flew back, tired from her busy night, Alice dropped off to sleep.

Alice woke in her own bed. She mistily remembered what had happened. Had she dreamed it all?

"Come on, Alice!" came a yell from downstairs. "Aunt Megan is waiting for her present."

Alice looked at the clock: half past nine! She leapt out of bed, grabbed her aunt's present, dashed downstairs and handed it over. As Aunt Megan was opening it, Alice remembered the tooth inside. She turned red and tried to think of an excuse to leave, but it was too late.

Aunt Megan opened the matchbox.

"Alice!" she said, her eyes widening. "How absolutely ... wonderful." She took from the box a pair of beautiful pearl earrings. "Put them on me, dear."

Alice did. When she looked at her aunt afterwards she thought, for the first time, that she wasn't so bad after all. "Out of the ordinary cometh the amathing," she lisped.

"Beg your pardon, dear?" said Aunt Megan.

"Oh, er, nothing," replied Alice. "Breakfatht anyone?"

THE SILLY-WILLIES

King Dominic lived all alone in a huge castle in a town, the name of which no one could ever remember. This particular day, his old friend Whizz the magician was visiting.

"It's the strangest thing," said the king after dinner. "My loyal subjects have been extraordinarily silly lately. Yet whenever anyone says they're silly, they get very upset. They're a right bunch of silly-billies."

"It sounds more like the Silly-Willies," said the magician. "Silly-Willies are naughty fairies who roam about, staying in different towns. They creep into bedrooms at night and whisper silly things to do into someone's ear. That person is then in a Silly-Willy spell. Leave it to me, tomorrow I'll get to the bottom of it."

Next day, Whizz put on his best magician's robe and sauntered into town. On his way he walked over a hill. On top, standing under a tree, were two very frightened men.

"What's the matter?" asked Whizz.

"We're worried," said one, quivering.

"See that apple," said the first, pointing to the only apple in the tree.

"Yes," said Whizz.

"Well, what if there was a dreadful snow storm?" said the man.

"... With a strong wind," said the second.

"... The apple would blow off the tree ..." said the first.

"... And roll down the hill ..." continued the second.

"... And as it rolled it would make a huge snowball ..."

"... And what if a small girl was standing in its way ..."

"... Wearing a thick balaclava so she couldn't hear anything ..."

"... And it squashed her," concluded the second. They looked at each other and burst into tears.

"It would be so terrible," they sobbed together.

"Yes," said Whizz. "But what if it didn't snow? After all, it is the middle of August. And anyway," he said, picking the apple and biting it. "What apple?" At this, they turned to him and said, "What do you know?" Then they walked off.

Whizz carried on. "That's definitely one case of the Silly-Willies," he muttered to himself. Suddenly, from inside a house he heard:

Thump-thump-thump-thump ... Crash! Ow!

Whizz knocked and went inside. In the bedroom upstairs was a man who had hung his trousers on a chest of drawers. He was trying to put them on by running up and jumping into them, but each time he crashed into the drawers, banging his knees painfully.

"Why don't you step into them and pull them up with your hands?" said Whizz.

"What do you know?" said the man, rudely. "You don't even wear trousers. Now if you'll excuse me ..." As Whizz left he heard:

Thump-thump-thump-thump ... Crash! Ow!

That was another case of the Silly-Willies – and he found lots more that day.

As Whizz was returning that night, he saw some people standing around the town pond, murmuring.

"What's the matter?" said Whizz.

"The moon's fallen into the pond," said a woman, pointing into the pond at a reflection of the moon.

"That's only its relection," said Whizz.

"What do you know, smarty-pants?" she said.

"I'll show you," he replied. He took a stick and stirred up the surface of the water, shattering the reflection into a million rippling fragments.

"He's broken the moon!" shouted a man.

"Get him!" said another. They chased Whizz all the way back to the castle.

That night, he told King Dominic all about his findings.

"What can we do?" said the king.

"Well," began Whizz. "The Silly-Willies get into people's bedrooms through keyholes. If everyone blocks them up, they'll move on somewhere else. As they aren't in the castle, you needn't bother."

The king issued a proclamation, and everyone blocked their bedroom keyhole. Next day, there were no cases of the Silly-Willies anywhere in the town. That night, Whizz was ready to move on.

"I can't thank you enough," said the king. Then as Whizz trotted off on his horse he added, "But where are the Silly-Willies now?"

"Who knows?" replied the magician. "The Silly-Willies come and go like the wind. They could be anywhere, absolutely anywhere. Thanks for having me. Goodbye."

The king watched his friend disappearing and then saw the drawbridge being raised. Suddenly, he stared with horror into the moat.

"Whizz!" he shouted with all his might. "Whizz! Come back! It's the moon! It's fallen into the moat!"

THE MAGICIAN'S ASSISTANT

Alex was a magician's assistant, although he hadn't learned any magic, yet. He assisted a magician called Madge, a good woman whose main aim was to find spells to cure people's ills and help them in various ways.

Madge's spell room was amazing. The walls were lined with all sorts of bottles and jars containing the strangest things you could imagine, and many you couldn't. There were also books, funny-shaped equipment, spiders' webs, dust, and the sort of grimy things that you find in places which haven't been properly cleaned for years.

One morning, Madge looked particularly excited. "It's time for magic," she said. "I need the Magispells book."

"I'll get it for you," chipped in Alex.

"Alex, you know I have told you never to go near my Magispells book. Magic is a serious business. I work only for good, but there is also nasty magic. Often the two are not that far apart."

Alex sulked. "When am I going to do some magic?" he grumbled. Madge ignored him and opened the enormous book. "Are you ready, Alexander?" Alex nodded and stood up lazily.

"I'm doing a specially whizzzy spell today – and that's 'whizzzy' with three 'Zs'. Now, let's see, I need some powdered chestnut, three tears of laughter and that caterpillar skin I asked you to drench in the beams of a full moon." Alex collected them and gave them to Madge.

"Thank you," she said, mixing them together.

"All I need now is some fluff from the pouch of a kangaroo." Alex went to the cupboard and looked at the jar.

"It's empty," he called.

"Oh tinkle," said Madge. "That means I'll have to go and borrow some from my friend Cuppen Sorcerer. I won't be long. Would you make a start on the clearing up please, but don't touch my spell. Toodle pipple." And she left. Alex looked at the mess and sighed.

"It's going to take me ages," he said to himself. Just then Catsby, Madge's cat, gave a loud miaow.

"You're right, Catsby," said Alex. "What a bore." Catsby purred and jumped onto the Magispells book. As Alex picked her up, he had an idea. There must be a tidying spell in the Magispells book. After all, he told himself, it would help Madge.

Alex opened the book and leafed through the pages. "Let's see, 'Cure For Hiccups' ... no, 'Spell To Turn Mud Into Chocolate' ... hmm, nice but not for now ... here we are: 'Tidying Up Spell'."

It looked quite easy really. He gathered the ingredients and mixed them together. Then came the magic words.

"*Ibblibum bottium, fattus wobblium ...* " he chanted. But Madge's handwriting was so hard to read that he started to make mistakes, "Er ... *capsicum sillius billium ...* is that *fillius dillium*?"

He was just about to give up when there was a huge thunderclap. Green smoke emerged from the book, wound itself in spirals and became a tall, green man with large, hairy ears. Alex was rooted to the spot.

"O most gracious master," said the creature, bowing. "I am your loyal servant, Hairylugs. Your wish is my command. You have but to ask. I am all ears."

"Mmm," Alex thought, "Your ears are pretty big." Then he said, "Great! Would you do a bit of tidying up for me, please?"

"No sooner said than done," said Hairylugs.

Alex had never seen anyone work so quickly. Hairylugs was like a green whirlwind. Jars flew back into place and bottles rattled onto their shelves. Alex smiled. "That'll show Madge," he thought.

"Now she'll have to let me do more magic."

Then things started to go a bit wrong. The creature started to tidy Madge's bench.

"No, leave that," said Alex. "That's enough." But Hairylugs just ignored him and carried on. Madge's new spell was swept into the waste bin. Then all the cobwebs and dust were brushed away, until the room was shining. Finally he picked up Catsby and put her away in a cupboard.

"What now, O master?" said Hairylugs.

"Er, nothing. You can go, thanks," replied Alex.

"What NEXT?" boomed Hairylugs.

Alex began to feel a bit scared, and well he might.

Because instead of calling a helpful fairy, he had called a mischievous goblin, who was now yelling, "I want an ORDER!"

Alex said the first job that come into his head, "Water the plants."

"No sooner said than done," said Hairylugs, but with a sneer rather than a smile. He went into the garden and poured gallons over each plant, so that the garden was awash. Then he came inside and started to water the house plants. He used a huge bucket, which he kept on filling and emptying over the pots with a great Sploosh!

"Stop! Stop!" said Alex, as the water started to rise over his ankles.

"Why?" bellowed Hairylugs. Sploosh! "I have to obey your command, you worm!" Sploosh! The water kept rising, and Alex began to cry.

"Ha! Ha!" laughed the goblin. "Trying to help me water with your tears?" Sploosh!

Suddenly, the door burst open and Splo-WOOSH! Madge was knocked over by a tidal wave.

She took one look at Alex's face and
Hairylugs' frantic activity and instantly
summoned up all her wisdom and fairy
knowledge. She took out her wand and
challenged Hairylugs to a battle of magic.
There were massive explosions as spells
fizzed and crackled all around. Alex crouched
behind the bench, wide-eyed as Madge and Hairylugs
changed each other into all sorts of amazing things.
Then Madge came across the waste bin containing
her spell. She took the kangaroo fluff from her pocket
and mixed it in.

She yelled the spell at Hairylugs, who instantly screamed, became a cloud of green smoke and disappeared up the chimney.

"Phew!" said Madge. "It was a good thing I was working on a spell to get rid of goblins."

Alex thought he was going to get the biggest scolding of his life, but Madge decided he'd learned his lesson well enough. All she said was, "You see, not much separates good magic from nasty magic; it can be as little as a badly made spell."

At this point, they both heard a scratching noise.

"Hairylugs!" screamed Alex, diving under a chair. Madge went over to a cupboard and opened it. Out skipped Catsby, who stretched, yawned and went to her bowl to remind everyone that it was time for dinner.

THE FAIRY AT THE WELL

Once there was a man who lived with his two sons. The elder, Oscar, was the spitting image of his father. This meant he was good-looking, grumpy and greedy.

The younger son, Kevin, was kindness itself. But the father treated Oscar like a prince and made Kevin do all the horrible jobs. Each morning, Kevin had to get up before the sun did and walk for two hours to fetch water from the well. When he got back he had to take Oscar breakfast in bed.

One day, while he was at the well, Kevin was approached by a scruffy, old woman. "May I have a drink, please?" asked the woman.

"Certainly," said Kevin. He pulled up the bucket of water and poured some into a jug for her.

The woman was really a fairy who had made herself poor to see just how kind Kevin was. She said, "From now on, with every word you say, a flower or precious stone will fall from your mouth."

When Kevin got home his father barked, "You're five minutes late."

"Yes, I'm sorry Dad," said Kevin. A diamond, two tulips and a ruby fell onto the kitchen floor.

"A-ma-zing!" said his father. Then he made Kevin tell him what had happened, which made more jewels and flowers come out of his son's mouth. When Kevin had finished, his father sent him to clean out the pigsty while he picked the jewels out of the wonderful pile on the floor. Then he called Oscar.

"There's an old woman down at the well," he said, his eyes burning with greed. "Give her some water and she'll give you something amazing."

"Do it yourself," said the incredibly rude son.

"Go, or you'll feel my shoe on your bottom," shouted his father. Oscar picked up the jug and stomped off.

By the time he reached the well he was hot and sweaty. He had just sat down when a young woman came up to him.

"Hello, sir," she said. "Would you kindly get me some water, please."

Oscar looked up. "Oh, Miss La-di-da wants some water, does she?" he said with a sneer. "Get it yourself."

The girl was the same fairy as before, only this time she wanted to see just how nasty Oscar was.

"Every word you speak shall turn into something horrible," said the fairy, and disappeared.

Oscar walked home without the jug. When he arrived his father said, "Did you meet her?"

"No, I didn't," puffed Oscar. Two rotten eggs and a dead beetle fell from his mouth.

"Ugh!" yelled the father. "This is Kevin's fault." Then he ran off to smack his younger son. However, Kevin heard him coming and left the house. He went to a big city, where his wealth could help the poor.

As for Oscar, he now had to do all the jobs around the house. He moaned so much that the house was soon filled with nasty things, so his father threw him out. The fairy went back to Queen Mab, the queen of the fairies, and sang her this song,

"A *person speaking gentle words,*
Spreads joy as great as jewels.
But nasty mouths are worth as much
As kindness is to fools."

THE DISOBEDIENT DOG

"Alfie, will you come here!" yelled Mr. Truffle at his disobedient dog. But Alfie just sat in the middle of the park and looked around at the beautiful summer's day.

Mr. Truffle walked on until he arrived at the gate, then he turned and shouted, "Alfie, come HERE!" Alfie sniffed the air, made a lazy snap at a passing bumble bee, then lay down on the grass. All the other people in the park looked and smiled, just as they did every day. It was quite entertaining to see Mr. Truffle getting angrier and angrier.

"Well, blow me down!" said Mr. Truffle, turning red. "Everyone else's dog obeys them, why can't mine?" He walked out of the gate in the direction of his house. When a minute had passed, Alfie got up and trotted happily after him.

Once more he'd shown everyone who was the boss.

"That dog! That dog!" puffed Mr. Truffle when he got home. He was just about to close the door, when Alfie walked in, sat down and started a long, slow scratch.

"And you can stop that!" shouted Mr. Truffle. But Alfie didn't, of course. He kept on showering the kitchen with hairs, bits of twig and grass.

"Well, blow me down!" said Mr. Truffle.

The following day, Mr. Truffle walked Alfie in the wood next to the park. He threw a stick, but Alfie just trotted off in the other direction, with a look which said, "Fetch it yourself". Suddenly, there was a bright flash and in front of Mr. Truffle appeared a small dog. It had a shiny gold collar and hovered above the ground using tiny silver wings.

"Hello," it said. "I'm your furry dogmother."

"Well, blow me down!" said Mr. Truffle.

"I'm from the land of pixie poodles, leprechaun labradors and spritely spaniels. Name a wish and it shall be done."

"I wish that Alfie would obey me," said Mr. Truffle, after no more than a second's thought.

"All right," said the fairy dog. It wagged its tail, causing a spray of shimmering stars to fall on Mr. Truffle. "He will now obey every single word you say." Then it was gone.

Mr. Truffle rubbed his eyes. "Well, blow me down!" he said again. "It must have been a dream."

He walked out of the wood into the park. "Come on Alfie," he said without thinking. The next thing he knew, there was a rumble of approaching paws as Alfie came rushing up and walked obediently at his master's side.

Mr. Truffle stopped in amazement.

"Are you feeling all right, Alfie?" he asked. Alfie stared at him, panting eagerly, looking as though he was waiting for a command. Mr. Truffle hardly dared say anything.

"Sit," he said at last. Alfie obeyed. "Lie down." Alfie obeyed. "Roll over." Again, Alfie obeyed. Mr. Truffle picked up a stick and threw it into the middle of the park. By now, people were starting to watch.

"Alfie ..." said Mr. Truffle. Alfie sat up, alert. "Alfie, fetch!" Alfie set off like a streak of lightning, and grabbed the stick with his mouth as he slid past. Then, his feet scampering wildly, he tore back to Mr. Truffle, dropped the stick at his feet, and sat waiting for his next order.

The people in the park could not believe it. Mr. Truffle could not believe it. He just scratched his head and said, "Well, blow me down!"

But unfortunately, the magic was still working. Alfie obeyed – and blew him down!

65

FAIRY NUFF

Fairy Nuff wasn't beautiful and graceful like other fairies, but thin and rather scruffy. As she was only a beginner fairy her magic was a disaster, but it never seemed to matter too much.

One day, there was great excitement in the part of Fairyland where she lived because Queen Mab, the queen of the fairies, was coming. Not surprisingly, everyone wanted to put on a good show for her.

"We could do a dance," said Appleblossom.

"I think we should sing," chirped Larkspur.

"What about a play?" said Skipwillow.

"Hmm," said Perriwiggin. "Fairy Nuff, what do you think we should do?"

"Well, how about a bit of everything?" she replied.

"Excellent," said Perriwiggin. "We'll take turns doing whatever we feel Queen Mab would like.

But we must keep this visit to ourselves. The hobgoblins would love to spoil it."

The next day, Fairy Nuff met her friend Catkin.

"I'm going to make a picture out of spiders' webs," said Catkin. "What about you?"

"It's a surprise," replied Fairy Nuff. "But I'll be using magic."

"The last time you used magic you turned all the trees into purple piglets by mistake," said Catkin.

"Whoops-a-buttercup," said Fairy Nuff, as she remembered. Then she set about arranging her surprise. She was going to do a spell which would write something in the sky, but what? She wandered along a path trying out some rhyme ideas:

"*Queen Mab, you are welcome,*
Here's some flowers, want to smell some?"

"Hmm, It's a bit long," she thought. Then she stopped and yelled, "*Queen Mab, you are fab* ... Brilliant!"

"What are you doing?" came a voice.

She looked and saw a crow sitting on a branch.

"It's a secret for Queen Mab," she said.

The crow's eyes lit up. "Really? When's she coming then?"

"I'm not allowed to tell you that it's this evening," said Fairy Nuff.

Unfortunately, the crow wan't really a crow at all. It was Gobby, the chief hobgoblin, who now scrambled down from the tree and ran home, chuckling. The hobgoblins were always looking for ways to annoy the fairies. Very soon, they had thought up a horrible plan to ruin the royal visit.

That evening, Queen Mab arrived in a beautiful water lily coach, which was pulled by dragonflies. The celebrations got underway. Hop-o-my-Thumb played her harp, Larkspur sang a song and Appleblossom danced on a large mushroom. There were many more wonderful things before Skipwillow, Acorncup and Merrywort performed a play about the fairies beating the hobgoblins at football. Everyone gathered around and cheered and clapped so loudly that no one noticed the hobgoblins creeping nearer.

"Come on," whispered Gobby. "We'll hide in the bushes behind this flowerbed. They won't be laughing for long."

There were muffled giggles from the others as they got their smelly-spells ready. These were spells which, when set off by magic, covered whoever was near them with a bright, slimy, gooey stuff which was stinkier than a mountain of old manure.

Back at the celebrations, Fairy Nuff was the last to perform. She leapt into the clearing, but was so excited that she tripped over a molehill. As she hit the ground, the spell shot out of her magic wand. It landed in the flowerbed near the hobgoblins and set everything off like fireworks. Bluebells, dandelions and daisies all whooshed up like rockets, and so did the hobgoblins.

There were great clouds of green, blue, silver, yellow – it was like a sparkling rainbow.

The smelly-spells went so high that the fairies couldn't smell them. But the hobgoblins could. They got covered in stinky stuff and shouted "Euuugh!" and "Phaaaaw!" and "Wheeew!" which from the ground sounded like firework noises. Eventually, all that could be seen in the sky were the words 'Queen Mab is fab.'

As the hobgoblins slunk off unseen, all scorched and smelly, Queen Mab said, "Thank you, Fairy Nuff. That's the best flowerwork display I've ever seen!"

FAIRY NUFF AND THE GOGGLE MONSTER

One morning, the people of the village of Great Wheezing awoke to a terrible calamity. Julia, the elder daughter of Old Barden, the village gardener, had disappeared. The grown-ups all milled about helplessly, trying to decide what to do (especially P.C. Fleeceman, the village policeman). Only Molly, Julia's little sister, knew what had happened. However, no one would listen to her, so she went to the wood outside the village and started to cry. Her sobs were interrupted by a wild screeching:

"Blue! I said BLUE!"

Molly looked behind a bush and saw a patch of what looked like bluebells, only they were bright red. In front of them was a fairy, waving a magic wand and yelling madly. The fairy was a little thin and rather plain and scruffy.

"Hello," said Molly. "I like your redbells."

The fairy spun around so quickly that she toppled over and dropped her wand, which fizzed madly.

"Whoops-a-buttercup," said the fairy. "Sorry, er, I'm Fairy Nuff."

"I'm Molly," said Molly, and burst into tears again. At this point, any other fairy would have been very cautious, but Fairy Nuff had a heart as kind as a summer's day. She listened as Molly told her all about her sister's disappearance. When she'd finished, Fairy Nuff said, "And you think you saw what happened?"

"I don't think, I know," said Molly. "She was grabbed by a huge moster with the most enormous eyes I've ever seen."

"*Goggle-Eyes!*" exclaimed Fairy Nuff. "He's horrible. He lives on a mountain somewhere near Iceland. His big, goggly eyes are special: he never has to go to sleep completely. He can always keep one open, which will make it very difficult to rescue Julia."

"What? Do you mean you'll rescue her?" said Molly.

"Of course," said Fairy Nuff. She didn't tell Molly that as she was a beginner fairy she wasn't supposed to attempt anything dangerous. But then, she was a rebel with a wand.

"Let's go!" she said, waving it bravely.

"To Iceland!"

After visiting Ireland, then Thailand, they eventually ended up in a cold cave.

"Are we a bit nearer to Goggle-Eyes this time?" said Molly.

"Who said that?" came a deep voice that boomed around the cave.

"Does that answer your question?" whispered Fairy Nuff.

"Aha! Supper!" said Goggle-Eyes. They saw two huge eyes looking at them. Next to him was a cage containing Julia. Fairy Nuff wasn't very quick, but when a monster is about to shake salt and pepper over you, you tend to think rather quickly.

"But we've got something for you," she said. Goggle-Eyes paused. Everyone likes a present, even hungry monsters.

"What is it?" he said.

"Er ... it's a ... erm ..." said Fairy Nuff. Then an idea struck her. "A concert," she said looking at Molly. "My friend Molly here is an amazing musician." Molly looked worried. The only music she ever played was on her CD player.

"Listen," said Fairy Nuff, thinking this spell:
"*Play, O music, close both his eyes,*
A flute to toot to beddy-byes."
Immediately in Molly's hands there appeared some
bagpipes. "Whoops-a-pansy," muttered Fairy Nuff.

Molly began to play the bagpipes and, with the
help of the magic, managed quite a good tune.

"Lovely!" said the monster. "It reminds me of
Grandpa Goggle MacGoggle. When I was a mini-
monster we used to dance before I went to bed."
Then the monster got up and jigged around the floor,
whooping madly. Far from sending him to sleep, he
was so enjoying himself his huge eyes were open
wider than ever.

When Molly had run out of breath, the monster said, "Right, now I'll have my supper."

"Is that what you did after you danced with your grandpa?" asked Fairy Nuff.

"Don't be stupid," said Goggle-Eyes. "It was bedtime, he used to tell me a story."

"Well that's your second surprise," said Fairy Nuff and immediately launched into a story. "Once upon a time, in a far-away land ..."

"Is it about Baby Goggle?" the monster interrupted.

"... Lived Baby Goggle," said the quick-thinking fairy. And she went on to tell a fantastic story in which Baby Goggle terrorized three whole villages and barbecued all their sheep. When she'd finished, there was loud snoring.

Fairy Nuff had worked an amazing trick. As the monster's eyes had been open incredibly wide during all the frantic music and dancing, they were now incredibly tired. So he had closed both of them for a quick nap.

Julia was rescued from the cage and, after two tries, Fairy Nuff managed to magic them all back to Great Wheezing. The delighted villagers held a huge party that evening, at which Fairy Nuff was the special guest. Just as she was about to make her speech, a messenger arrived from Queen Mab, the queen of the fairies.

"Attention!" he said. "Queen Mab says that Fairy Nuff is no longer a beginner fairy. She will be responsible for looking after this village from now on." There was a huge cheer, especially from Molly and Julia.

Fairy Nuff stood on the table and said, "You don't need to worry any more about Goggle-Eyes. He'll be so embarrassed that he won't dare show up around here again. Still, to be on the safe side, you'd better keep your eyes open."

THE VINEGAR BOTTLE WOMAN

Once there was a woman called Mrs. Funnybones, who lived in a vinegar bottle. One day, a fairy was fluttering past the bottle when she heard Mrs. Funnybones talking and muttering to herself.

"Dear-oh-dearie me," she moaned. "Fancy me living in a mere vinegar bottle. I ought to live in a pretty little cottage with a thatched roof and roses around the front door."

The fairy, who was called Skip, was a kind creature. She listened to Mrs. Funnybones' complaints, and then she said,

"Just shout 'Wazoomer!', blink your eyes,
Tomorrow morning, big surprise."

Then she vanished in a cloud of fairy dust.

Mrs. Funnybones did as she was told, and the next morning she awoke in the prettiest little cottage you could imagine. She rushed outside and admired the thatched roof and the roses around the front door. Mrs. Funnybones was very happy in her little cottage. Every morning she went into her garden to smile at the rising sun. She also kept a hen, which laid a fresh egg every day for her breakfast.

Some time later, Skip the fairy decided to look in on Mrs. Funnybones to make sure everything was all right. When she got there, Mrs. Funnybones started complaining again.

"Dear-oh-dearie me. Fancy me living in a mere cottage. I ought to live in a house on a busy street, with people passing by and admiring the big, brass door knocker."

Skip listened patiently, then said,

"Just shout 'Wazoomer!', blink your eyes,
Tomorrow morning, big surprise."

Mrs. Funnybones did as she was told, and in the morning she found herself in a bigger bed, in a bigger house. Through the open window she heard a passer-by say,

"Wow! Look at that amazing big, brass door knocker!"

She loved her house, and she kept it clean and tidy. People in her street often popped in for tea. She walked to the supermarket every day and bought

eggs, bread and orange juice for her breakfast.

Some time later Skip was passing by the house again, when she heard Mrs. Funnybones' voice saying,

"Dear-oh-dearie me. Fancy me living in a mere house. I ought to be living in a mansion with a lake in the garden."

Again, Skip listened, then said,

"Just shout 'Wazoomer!', blink your eyes,
Tomorrow morning, big surprise."

Sure enough, Mrs. Funnybones awoke the next morning in a beautiful four-poster bed, in a huge mansion. She had a large garden with a lake. She also had eggs, bread, mushrooms, tomatoes, bacon and sausages, delivered every day for her breakfast.

Skip was sure that this time Mrs. Funnybones would by happy, but no! Not long after, as she was flying through the mansion garden, she heard a sad voice from the edge of the lake.

"Dear-oh-dearie me. Fancy me living in a mere mansion. I ought to live in a palace and be a queen, with lots of servants." Skip couldn't believe her ears. But her disbelief wasn't as great as her kindness, so she said,

"Just shout 'Wazoomer!', blink your eyes,
Tomorrow morning, big surprise."

Mrs. Funnybones became Queen Mrs. Funnybones. She did lots of queenie things, such as open buildings, launch ships, meet important visitors and travel to foreign lands.

She also had servants to bring her breakfast in bed: orange juice, eggs, bread, mushrooms, tomatoes, bacon and sausages.

A short while later, flitting past the palace, Skip heard something which almost made her wings wither.

"Dear-oh-dearie me. Fancy me being a mere queen of one country. I ought to be the Ruler of the World."

Skip sighed and said again, (altogether now),
"Just shout 'Wazoomer!', blink your eyes,
Tomorrow morning, big surprise."

When she awoke next morning, Mrs. Funnybones had the biggest surprise of all. She was back in her vinegar bottle. It was exactly the same, except for a small globe Skip had put there so Mrs. Funnybones could rule over the world to her heart's content.

THE NOSE TREE

Wendy held on to the stolen doughnut, ran deep into the wood, and sat down. Something stirred nearby, and, to her great surprise, she saw it was a sleeping fairy. Instantly, she forgot about the doughnut and carefully caught the fairy by the arm, waking her up.

"Oh no," said the little creature. "I must learn not to go to sleep outside Fairyland." She started to cry, so Wendy took pity on her and released her grip.

The fairy stopped crying and said, "At least I'm not as silly as you. If you'd held on to me for a week, I would have had to grant you any wish you liked." It was now Wendy's turn to cry. She was very poor, and a fairy wish would have been very welcome.

"Oh, all right," said the fairy. "I will give you something after all."

The fairy waved her hand, and Wendy's doughnut moved all by itself, became a silver bracelet and slipped itself over her wrist.

"It glows when magic's around," said the fairy, and she vanished.

A few days later, Wendy's travels took her to a large city. Everyone was lining the main street. After a while, a procession came along.

"That's lucky, I've come on a carnival day," said, Wendy to a woman nearby.

"We do this every day," she groaned. "It's Prince Handsome. We all have to look at him. Mind you do."

As the procession came close, Wendy saw a man in an elegant coach. He certainly was handsome, and he knew it, because he was looking at himself in a golden mirror. Just then, Wendy noticed a doughnut in the road, about to be squashed. As she bent to pick it up, she heard a thin but stern voice.

"Stop! There's someone who is not looking at my radiant beauty," said the prince.

"Guards! Arrest her at once!" he said.

Wendy was taken back to the palace and left alone in a room. After a while, she noticed that her bracelet was glowing. It got brighter as she moved nearer to a cupboard. Wendy looked inside and saw the fairy who had given her the bracelet. She was in a glass box with a huge padlock.

"I fell asleep again," said the fairy. "The prince caught me. In a few more days he'll have a wish."

"What will he wish for?" asked Wendy.

It was the prince himself who answered her, "To rule the world!" His eyes were bright with power-craziness.

"I will wish that everyone in the world must adore my wondrousness, and be my slaves forever,"

Wendy knew that she must get away from the castle, so she said, "Beware, Prince. See my bracelet glowing! Its magic powers will spoil your plan." At this, the prince thought it would be best if she wasn't around any longer.

"You may go, but if I ever see you again, I'll send you to prison for a thousand years."

Once away from the city, Wendy wandered around the forest until she noticed that her bracelet was glowing again. She looked up and saw a strange-looking tree, heavy with huge, shiny apples. She ate one, and her nose grew to an enormous length.

"Thanks, bracelet," she said with a huff. It was still glowing, and she saw that next to the apple tree was a pear tree. "Oh well, I'll try these," she said. "Who knows, they may give me ears as big as parachutes." She ate a pear, and her nose grew back to the normal size again. Then, she had a brilliant idea.

Disguising herself as an old woman, Wendy went back to the city with a basket of magic apples. Just before the prince's procession, she put the basket on the roadside. The people were so busy looking at the prince they didn't see it, but he did.

"What splendiferous apples," he said. "I can see my gorgeous face in them, so they must be pretty amazing. Bring them to the palace for my lunch."

Back in the forest, Wendy put some pears into a bag and, still disguised, went back to the city.

At the castle, Wendy amazed the guards by knowing there was something wrong with the prince. She said she was the only doctor who could cure him. The courtyard where the prince had eaten the apples was now full of his nose.

"My magnificent looks! Ruined!" he wailed.

"Hmm," said Wendy. "It's the worst case of Conkitis since Pinocchio. I would hate to be around when you sneeze."

"What can I do?" said the prince in despair.

"Well, I recommend that you sleep in the pond tonight," said Wendy. "Would you like a pear in case you feel midnight peckish?"

In the pond, the prince ate the pear. Next morning, his fingers were crinkly, but his nose was shorter.

"But it still reaches all the way around the palace," he said. "Twice."

"Sit on the castle wall in your underpants," said Wendy. "Fancy a few pears to eat up there?"

The prince sat on the wall (which the people thought was very funny) and ate the pears. By lunchtime his nose was only twenty feet long.

"Shall I stay longer?" he said. "My bottom's a bit cold, but I don't mind."

"No," said Wendy. "There is only one way to get your nose finally back to size."

"How?" he said. "I'll do anything, anything at all."

"Release the fairy," said Wendy.

"But I want to rule the world," he said.

"With a twenty foot nose?" said Wendy.

Prince Handsome released the fairy.

"I shall make your nose the right size," she said. "But if you ever say how good-looking you are, it will grow to super-elephant proportions again."

Then she looked at Wendy. "Thank you very much. Enjoy your doughnut." She disappeared.

Wendy noticed that her bracelet had fallen to the floor and was now a doughnut again.

"I bet it's a magic one," said Prince Handsome.

Wendy ate half of it and, as she swallowed, the doughnut grew back so that it was whole again.

"It's a never-ending one," she said. "How clever of you to know. You must have a nose for magic."

CRAFTY HERBERT

Strange things sometimes happened in the village of Bomford. Once, a park bench had suddenly turned into a huge chocolate ice cream, which wasn't very pleasant for the person sitting on it at the time. It was always Crafty Herbert's fault.

Crafty Herbert was a particular type of fairy, known as a shape-shifter. This meant he could become anything he wanted in the blink of an eye.

On the edge of the village lived a woman called Nancy. She had a small cottage with a garden as pretty as a box of paints. She spoke kindly to the flowers and always watered them well. This pleased the fairies, who made sure that the flowers lasted an extra-long time.

Crafty Herbert was not pleased though. He got fed up with hearing the fairies chattering about how sweet Nancy was, always so cheerful and kind. So he set out to do something about it.

One day, Nancy went to milk her cow, called Moo.
She didn't know that Crafty Herbert had hidden her
cow and turned himself into one exactly the same.

"Hello Moo my darling," said Nancy, sitting on her
stool and putting her bucket underneath the cow's
udder. She was just about to start milking when the
cow walked forward.

"What are you doing?" asked Nancy, moving her
stool and bucket. But as she sat down the cow
stepped back to where it was at the beginning.
Normally, it took Nancy half an hour to milk Moo.
Today, it took three hours.

"Well, I'll be a marmalade milk-churn, what's come
over you?" she said, picking up the bucket.

"Well, I know what's going to come over you,"
thought Crafty Herbert, and he kicked the bucket in
Nancy's hand so that the milk went all over her.

Nancy was speechless with rage. She turned and
walked briskly back to her house, hardly noticing the
muffled sound of mooey laughter.

Tricks such as this went on for weeks, until Nancy could stand it no more. She went to see the Wise Woman, who lived in a cave just outside the village.

When Nancy had finished telling her tale, the Wise Woman said, "It's old Crafty Herbert. I'm as sure as ducks are quackers." And she told Nancy all about the fairy and his shape-shifting tricks. "He's like magic clay," she said.

"But how can I stop him?" said Nancy.

"He only plays tricks when he knows it's annoying someone. He hates all laughter but his own," said the Wise Woman. "So, beat him at his own game."

Nancy spent all of the next day working in her strawberry patch. She was just bending down to pull up some weeds underneath the scarecrow, when the scarecrow (who was really you-know-who) turned into a bag of flour, which burst all over poor Nancy. Her first reaction was to scream with rage, but then she remembered what the Wise Woman had said and roared with laughter.

"Another wonderful trick!" she guffawed. Crafty Herbert, who had been running away disguised as a puff of wind, suddenly stopped. He looked at Nancy and her laughing face, and he started to scowl.

"Wonderful tricks? Aren't you angry then?" he asked.

"Angry? They've made my life so full of surprises, I never know what's coming next."

Crafty Herbert was just going off in a sulk when something made him stop. Two boys from another village were passing and had watched Nancy speaking. As Herbert was disguised as a puff of wind, they'd thought Nancy was talking to herself.

"Look at that silly old woman, Gary," said one.

"She's talking to thin air, Barry," said the other. "And she's covered in flour. She's so stupid, she wouldn't notice if we had her strawberries." They pushed their way into the garden and started to stuff their pockets with fruit.

Now Crafty Herbert was naughty, but he wasn't nasty like these louts. When they weren't looking, he turned himself into two beautiful girls.

"Hello mother, hello boys," said one.

The boys stared, with their mouths open so wide that the strawberry juice ran down their chins. Nancy was speechless.

"Fancy coming to the fair with us?" said the other, with a smile. Then the girls turned and walked out of the front gate, beckoning to the boggle-eyed bullies. The boys forgot the strawberries and fell over each other to get at the gate. They walked with the girls for ages until eventually it began to get dark.

"It's just across this field," said the girls, opening a gate. The boys leapt over the wall to show off, and instantly sunk up to their waists in a slimy, wet bog.

The girls each grabbed a boy and started to pull.

When the boys were nearly out, a very strange thing happened. The girls began to merge together. Then before you could say "soggy underpants" each boy found himself holding a hand of Crafty Herbert, who began to laugh loudly. The boys were absolutely scared out of their wits.

"It's a ghost, Gary!" cried Barry.

"It's a monster, Barry!" cried Gary.

"RUN!" they cried together.

They scampered off in opposite directions, and didn't find each other for three months.

As for Nancy, she lived quietly and happily in her little cottage, and quite undisturbed by mischievous fairies, for the rest of her days.